Sam's BACK!

• Cartoons by John Howcroft •

The Five Mile Press

The Five Mile Press Pty Ltd
22 Summit Road
Noble Park Victoria 3174
Australia

Printed in Australia

Some people say
it's lonely out here.

 But I don't.

I might though.

If there was someone
to say it to .

A lovely spring day
and _look_ what she's wearing.

Here comes the shearing muster
three bikes,
a four by four truck,
ten sheepdogs and
a blue heeler with mange.

Why would God bother making those dreadful dogs.?

Goodness Knows.

He was self-taught you Know.

That explains it.

Remind me to renegotiate
the Sheepdog Limitation Treaty.

Don't worry, they're only day-trippers.

Would you care to join us Sam?
We need one more for a flock.

I'm not moving until I see
your dog licence.

Look! He's wearing
our favourite
sheepdog expression.

— sit

Can you come back later ?
He's at lunch.

It's too hot for shearing.
Didn't you get my memo ?

I suppose you are all wondering
why I sent for you.

Stay there and I'll find
a sheep for you to chase.

You can't trust those
sheepdogs —
they're masters of
disguise.

When the Kelpie barks.

I want you all to run towards the woolshed.

Now we're on our feet,
let's have some exercises
to tighten-up those
tummy muscles.

If you could only see
how ridiculous you look.

That's not your father
he was much taller.

This is your Kelpie speaking.
Our estimated time of arrival
at the shearing shed is 4pm.
We hope you enjoy
the journey.

  — We'll be stopping at the dam for a drink soon.

I hope —
I can get a
milk thistle
there.

 You're not pregnant again are you?

What's it like in ?

If it's not a vintage Cadillac
we could be in trouble.

Let's go —
my toes are wrinkly.

Stand back —
or he'll shake all over you.

1

You've had enough to drink.
Come and meet the Border Leicesters.

Let's give this communal living the flick
and go off somewhere on our own.

Hey !!

Look what I found .!

1
E-y-e-s-
right !!

A ram wants to Know if
we pay travelling expenses.

For goodness sake
do something about
your halitosis.

OK! POINT TAKEN.

Not – too – short –
because – of – a – sniffle.
Just let me run that
past the shearer.

How about William at 11.30 ?

Do you come here often?

Aren't you getting
too close to the client.?

If there's anything
in reincarnation —
I might do this to you
one day.

Would you like to come up
and see my crutchings?

Now that we've got the gear off
let's try some skinny dipping.

Sorry I'm not laughing.
But there are times
when it's hard to appreciate a good joke.

Blast! The mailman has done
the crossword again.

Once you're on a mailing list
there is no escape.

The card in front of you
shows the safety features
of this vehicle.
Please take a moment
to study them.

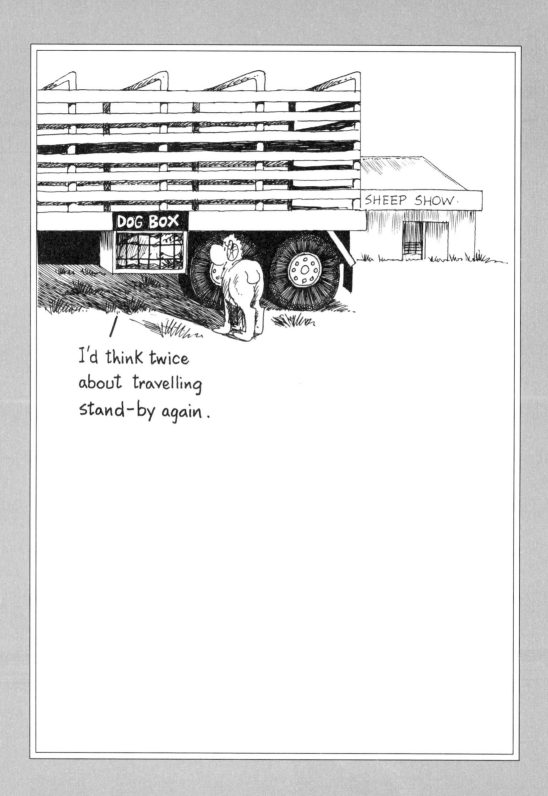

I'd think twice
about travelling
stand-by again.

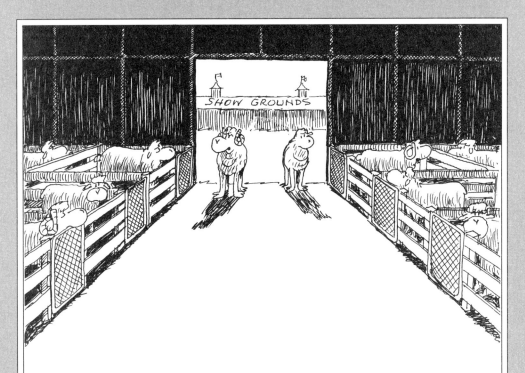

They didn't say anything
about sharing.

It's not fair !
I won the prize
but missed the
simple quiz question.

It makes you look fat.

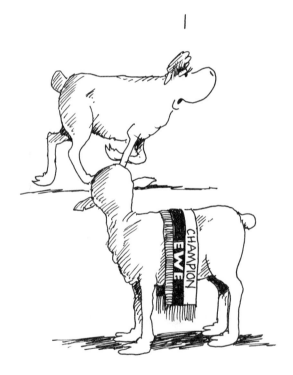

It's about time they were brought to justice.

What was it you won Dear —
Champion Ram and what else ?

What a nerve
Keeping us up all night
looking at their show ribbons.

Spring is here
the grass is riz

I wonder where
the ewe flock iz .

I'm Sam
a Champion Ram.
Would you be interested in
a free introductory offer?

Send me a brochure.

Let's do lunch .!
I've found a stunning
little hole in the fence.

There's a precocious little clover in here
with a marvellous after-taste.

What a coincidence.
The Border Leicesters are eating here too.

We had an old Roller
when I was in the Western District.

Is it naturally curly
or do you do something to it ?

What a sleaze !
You can feel his eyes shearing you.

You've been misinformed —
I'm not too old to be considered effective

I'm too effective to be considered old.

Can't you talk about anything else but
spring and a sheep's libido?

Ah Ha !!
I knew there were other women .

Do you know anything about
a Shakespearean Festival
around here ?

What is it with you ?
You never strain on the chain
you never keep us awake
with your barking.

Settle down —
There'll be another one
in twenty minutes.

He was a creature with simple tastes..
a little saltbush, some dam water,
a milk-thistle on special occasions.

1

Hullo !
I haven't seen you for ages.

Look Nigel !
The ram's in the garden again.